D0260340
000003054987

First published in 2020 by Scholastic Children's Books
Euston House, 24 Eversholt Street, London NW1 1DB
a division of Scholastic Ltd

www.scholastic.co.uk
London · New York · Toronto · Sydney · Auckland
Mexico City · New Delhi · Hong Kong

ISBN 978 1407 19703 6
C&F ISBN 978 0702 30321 0

Printed in China

1 3 5 7 9 10 8 6 4 2

FSC www.fsc.org
MIX
Paper from responsible sources
FSC® C008047

LLAMA GLAMARAMA

Simon
James
Green

Illustrated by
Garry
Parsons

In Larry's barn,
the llamas were good.
They followed the rules,
they did as they should.

The llamas were calm,
their voices stayed low.
They made their way slowly
wherever they'd go.

Yes, Larry was proper
and very polite.
But he had a BIG SECRET
that happened at night.

He kept it all quiet
to avoid any drama, but
while the others all slept
he was ...

... A TOE-TAPPIN'

hand-clappin'

DAZZLIN'

DANCIN'

LLAMA!

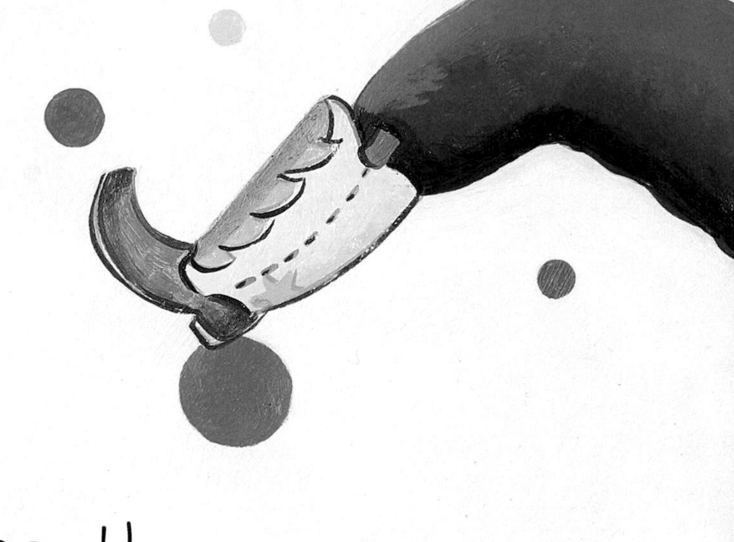

He loved to twist!

He stamped his feet!

He kept in time with the techno beat!

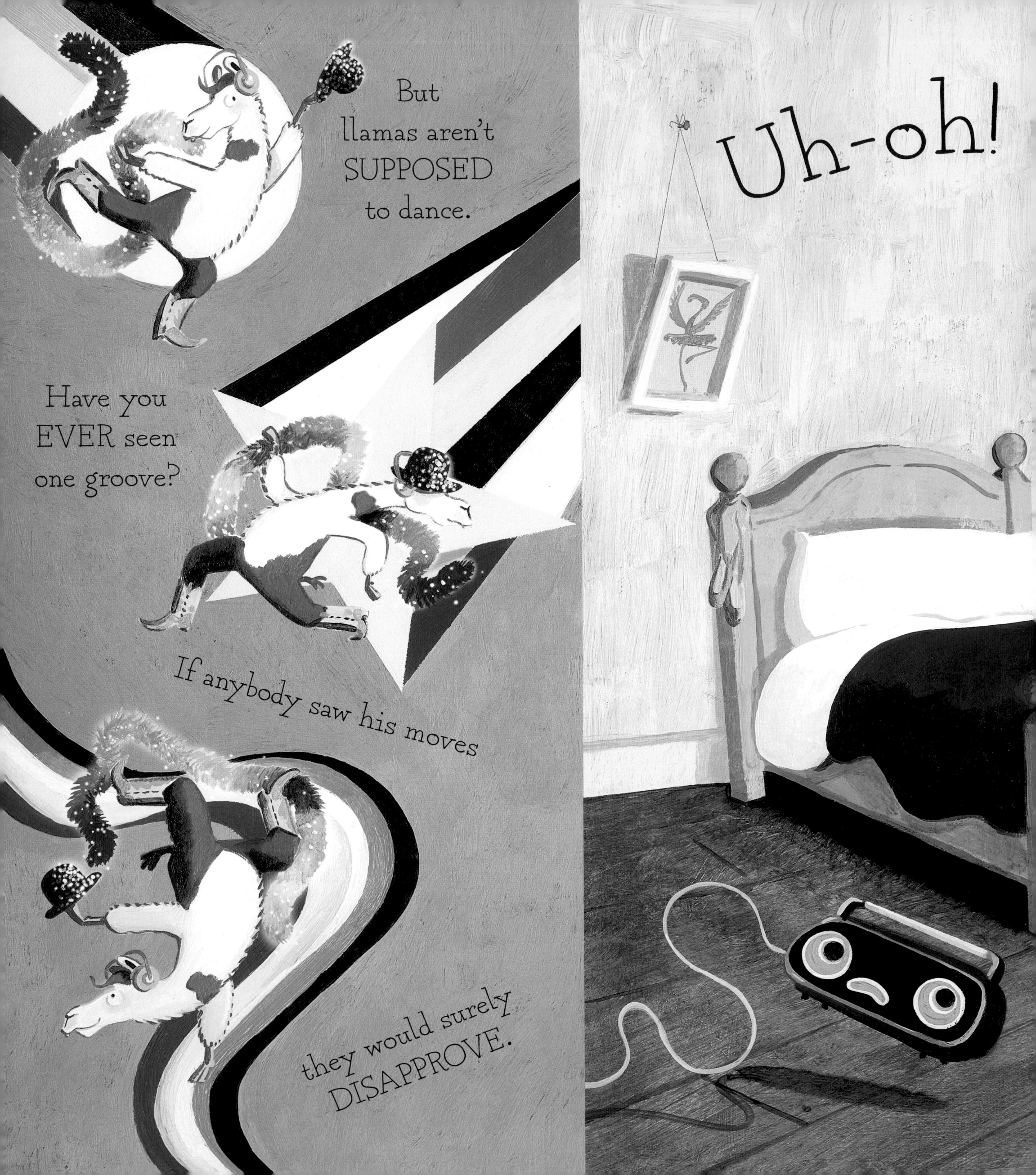
But
llamas aren't
SUPPOSED
to dance.
Have you
EVER seen
one groove?
If anybody saw his moves
they would surely
DISAPPROVE.
Uh-oh!

Someone's coming!
Stop the music! Hide the hat!
Jump in bed,
pretend to nap!

... but that would
never happen!"

"What?!
No way!" Larry said,
"I was just about to snooze!"

Spitz looked over at the bedpost.
"Do you have ... *ballet* shoes?"

"Err, *shoes*, you say?
That can't be!
I've been using these for ...
drinking tea?"
"But ..."

"... you don't
LIKE tea!"

"Oh, look! By that chair!
Are those APPLES over there?"

And while the others
turned away,

Larry made his getaway.

As he trudged down the lane, Larry was sad.
Being different was lonely.
Being different felt ... *bad.*

None of his friends liked to shimmy and flit.
Maybe the dance was a thing he should ... quit?

BUT
WHAT'S THIS?
A carnival?
Music?
FREE APPLES?!
The
Llama
DANCING!
FREE APPLES.
MUSIC!
SEE YOU AT THE
FAIRGROUND!

"Farewell, my friends! I bid adieu!
I'm going far away.* Please don't try to stop me.
I won't be back today..."

*In fact, he was only going down the road, and would definitely be back by teatime.

There in the distance: bold colours! Bright light!
For a lonely young llama, a spectacular sight!

Larry took a deep breath
and joined in the crowd.
He saw llamas *dancing*!
And the music was LOUD!

He grooved and he moved!
He leapt and he pranced!
Locking and popping, he loved the hip-hopping!

Salsa!

Flamenco!

Did he *belly dance*?

Flossing and tango, the jive and fandango!

He ate apples all day,
and met Llama Del Ray!
Loved hearing her sing.
He felt like a king!
LLAMAHA

Larry was HAPPY:
there were others like him!
The Llama Glamarama
was a WONDERFUL
THING!

He returned to the barn later that day.

"Listen up, friends, I've something to say.
I'm a little bit nervous, I'm taking a chance.

I hope you won't hate me,
but … I love to …
DANCE?"

Spitz raised an eyebrow.

Patch seemed to frown.

"Uh-oh," thought Larry,
"I'll have to leave town."

Then Spitz started ...

... giggling,

and Patch cracked a smile,

while Mop began clapping,

for quite

a long while!

It turned out that each
was a bit different too.

Patch's patch
was just *hair dye*
– really, it's true!

Spitz then
revealed that
he played
the maracas,

and Mop told the group
he was an alpaca!
(Everyone acted surprised,
but they had suspected this for a while.)

Larry showed his moves,
and all four danced with glee.
He sang: "I'm a rootin' tootin' lockin' poppin' groovin'

movin' llama,
and I'm proud to be ...
ME!

PURE
SILK
BECOMING
ALPACA